My Classic Stories

Jack and the Beanstalk

This book belongs to

Age -----------

*Enjoy this book,
love from* Jack

D0585178

This edition first published in 2013 by Ginger Fox Ltd
Copyright © 2013 Ginger Fox Ltd

Published in the UK by:
Ginger Fox Ltd
Stirling House, College Road
Cheltenham GL53 7HY
United Kingdom

www.gingerfox.co.uk

Retold by Nina Filipek
Illustrated by Bruno Merz

All rights reserved. No part of this work may be reproduced, stored in a
retrieval system, or transmitted in any form or by any means, electronic,
mechanical, photocopying, recording or otherwise, without the prior written
permission of the copyright owner.

ISBN: 978-1-909290-01-3

10 9 8 7 6 5 4 3 2 1

Printed and bound in China.

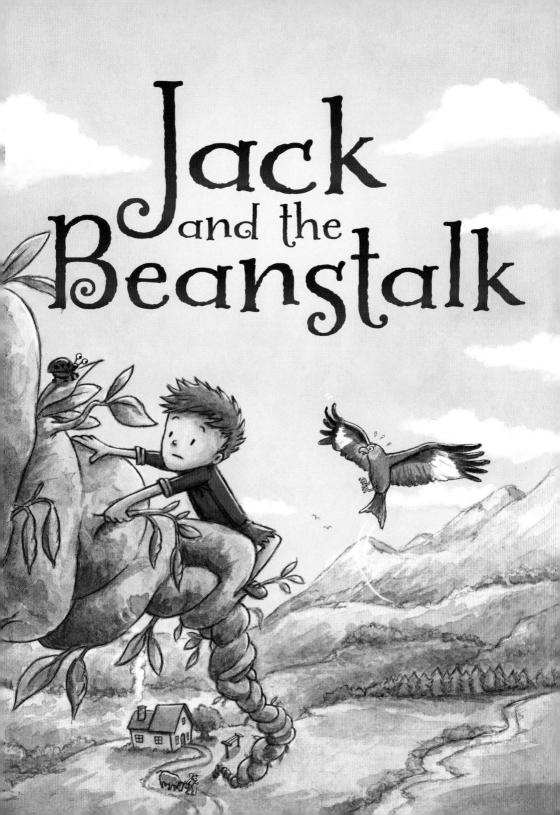

Jack
and the
Beanstalk

Once upon a time there was a boy called Jack who lived with his mother.

They lived in a little house in the countryside, where they owned a cow, but they were very poor.

One day, Jack's mother said,
"Take the cow to market and sell her
for as much money as you can."

Jack had not gone far before he met an old man.

"I'll give you five beans for your cow," said the old man.

"Five beans!" replied Jack.

"Why would I want five beans?"

"These are magic beans!" replied the old man.
"They will bring you luck."

Jack was excited at the thought of magic beans, so he gave the cow to the old man and took them.

When Jack got home, his mother
was very angry.

"You sold the cow
for five beans!" she shouted.
"Now we have nothing!"

She threw the beans
out of the window
and sent Jack to bed
without any supper.

10

But the beans really **were** magic, and during the night they started to grow.

The next morning when Jack woke up there was a **giant** beanstalk outside his window!

Before his mother could stop him, Jack climbed up to the top of the beanstalk! There he saw the most magnificent castle.

He went inside to look around. Then he heard a fierce voice,

"Fee, fi, fo, fum,
I smell the blood
of an
Englishman!
Be he alive

or be
he dead,
I'll grind his
bones to make
my bread!"

It was a **terrible ogre!**

Quickly, Jack hid in a cupboard. The ogre searched the castle but he could not find Jack.

The ogre gave up looking, and put a hen on the table.

"Lay!" bellowed the ogre, banging his fist.

The hen laid an egg – not an ordinary egg but a

golden egg!

The ogre then ate a huge meal and fell asleep in his chair.

Jack saw his chance. He picked up the hen and ran for the door.

"Help, Master!" clucked the hen.

The ogre woke up
and ran after Jack but,
quick as a flash,

Jack
slid

down

the

beanstalk.

Jack was so fast the ogre did not see
where he went.

Jack's mother was cross but she could not
stay angry for long when she saw the hen
lay a golden egg.

A few days later, when his mother was out, Jack climbed up the beanstalk again!

Jack tiptoed into the ogre's kitchen and hid in the cupboard once more. The ogre was sat at the table, counting golden coins.

"Fee, fi, fo, fum,
I smell the blood
of an
Englishman!

Be he alive or be
he dead,

I'll grind his bones

to make my

bread!"

The ogre searched the castle, but again
he could not find Jack. He put his magic
golden harp on the table.

"Play!"
bellowed the ogre,
banging his fist.

As the harp began to play it
sent the ogre quickly to sleep.

Jack saw his chance. He picked up the harp and ran for the door.

"Help, Master!"
sang the harp.

The ogre woke up immediately.

He saw Jack running towards the
beanstalk and chased after him.

Jack slid
    down the
        beanstalk.

            But this time
                the ogre
                followed.

"Mother!
Fetch the axe!"
cried Jack.

As soon as his feet
touched the ground,
Jack took the axe and
with one mighty chop he
split the beanstalk in two.

The terrible ogre came crashing down,
and that was the end of him!

Now that Jack and his mother had a hen
that laid golden eggs, and a magic harp,
they were no longer poor.

They lived
happily ever after.

Can you remember?

Now that you have read the story, try
to answer these questions about it.

1. What did the man give
   Jack in return for the cow? Was it:

   ## five beans?

   ## OR

   ## five pence?

2. What did Jack see when
   he woke up the next morning?

3. What was at
   the top of
   the beanstalk?

4. What did the ogre say when he
   was looking for Jack?

5. Did the magic beans bring Jack luck?

Did you spot?

Jack was very sneaky in the ogre's castle.
Did you spot anything else that sneaked into
the story? See if you can find what
else was there.

1. Did you see the seven mice?

2. Can you find a little beetle?

3. Where was the creepy-crawly spider?

4. Did you see what was
    in the picture at Jack's house?

5. What pattern was on
    the man's bag?

6. "Who is
hiding in my
hat?"

7. "Where did
I hide from
the ogre?"

My Classic Stories

Complete your collection ...

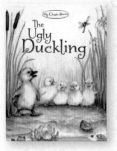

The Ugly Duckling

The Three Billy Goats Gruff

Hansel and Gretel

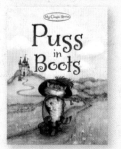

Puss in Boots

Little Red Riding Hood

Jack and the Beanstalk

Cinderella

The Gingerbread Man

The Emperor's New Clothes

Goldilocks and the Three Bears

Rapunzel

The Three Little Pigs

"Which one will you read next?"